Life Unshackled

From Darkness to Light

Mallikarjun B. Mulimani

Leadstart
INKSTATE

ISBN 978-93-90040-20-9
Copyright © Mallikarjun B. Mulimani, 2020

First published in India 2021 by Leadstart Inkstate
A Division of One Point Six Technologies Pvt Ltd

Sales Office:
Unit No.25/26, Building No.A/1,
Near Wadala RTO,
Wadala (East), Mumbai – 400037 India
Phone: +91 969933000
Email: info@leadstartcorp.com
www.leadstartcorp.com

All rights reserved. No part of this publication may be reproduced, stored in or introduced into a retrieval system, or transmitted, in any form, or by any means (electronic, mechanical, photocopying, recording or otherwise) without the prior written permission of the publisher. Any person who does any unauthorised act in relation to this publication may be liable to criminal prosecution and civil claims for damages.

Disclaimer: The views expressed in this book are those of the Author and do not pertain to be held by the Publisher.

Editor: Vaibhav Pathare
Cover: Ami Parekh
Layouts: Kshitij Dhawale

To,

All the Krupas and Rudras out there.

Foreword

Life Unshackled is the story of Rudra who is a victim of a dysfunctional milieu's conditionings and circumstances that wreck his early childhood, education, and career until the time he finds Krupa, a commercial sex worker, in whose company he finds solace and eventually falls in unconditional love with, which transforms their lives. It is also a story of a young man who successfully overcomes his miseries, manages to shape his career and life, and finally becomes unleashed from the web of life's thorny intricacies.

The book is also about the problems of life many individuals face in the system and how some overcome them eventually finding meaning in their lives. At the same time it is interesting to read and enjoy.

Prof. S. K. Saidapur

Educationist & Former Vice-Chancellor

Karnatak University Dharwad

About the Author

Mallikarjun B. Mulimani is a versatile writer. He writes novellas, novels, long and short poems including haikus. His books and style of writing, where brevity is the hallmark, influenced by his Engineering background, are unique and highly acclaimed. His writings are crisp, carrying a theme and a message making them highly readable. So far he has seventeen books to his credit. They revolve around diverse themes: psychology of humans and their milieu, God, love, sex, religion, realization of self, life, and death. They often touch the metaphysical domain.

Books by Author

1. Approaching Death
Writers Workshop, Kolkata, 2019

❖ ❖ ❖

2. A Mariachi & A Philosopher On Wheels – A Poem
Leadstart Publishing Pvt. Ltd., Mumbai, 2019

❖ ❖ ❖

3. A Writer's Zen
Leadstart Publishing Pvt. Ltd., Mumbai, 2018

❖ ❖ ❖

4. Selene – A Poem
Leadstart Publishing Pvt. Ltd., Mumbai, 2017

❖ ❖ ❖

5. Poems For Us
Leadstart Publishing Pvt. Ltd., Mumbai, 2017

❖ ❖ ❖

6. Poems To Myself
Leadstart Publishing Pvt. Ltd., Mumbai, 2017

❖ ❖ ❖

7. Alternative Haikus
Leadstart Publishing Pvt. Ltd., Mumbai, 2017

❖ ❖ ❖

8. Buddha In A Mercedes
Leadstart Publishing Pvt. Ltd., Mumbai, 2017

❖ ❖ ❖

9. Politics – A love Story
Leadstart Publishing Pvt. Ltd., Mumbai, 2016

❖ ❖ ❖

10. Bhakti Sans Religion – Dilemmas in the Search of One's True Inner Self

Leadstart Publishing Pvt. Ltd., Mumbai, 2016

❖ ❖ ❖

11. Star Ride to Nirvana

Leadstart Publishing Pvt. Ltd., Mumbai, 2015

❖ ❖ ❖

12. Dams across the Flow

Writers Workshop, Kolkata, 2015

❖ ❖ ❖

13. Victims Incorporated – Circles of Sub-consciousness

Current Publications, Agra, 2013

❖ ❖ ❖

14. What Happened to My Creativity

CreateSpace, USA, 2013

❖ ❖ ❖

15. Operation Epiphany – God's Journey on Earth

Writers Workshop, Kolkata, 2012

❖ ❖ ❖

16. The Holy Plumber and Other Stories

Writers Workshop, Kolkata, 2009

❖ ❖ ❖

17. Abstractions

Writers Workshop, Kolkata, 2007 (With digital art)

Acknowledgements

I am grateful to my teachers and well-wishers for their love and encouragement in writing this book.

Preface

Life Unshackled *From Darkness to Light* is a work that deals with the action and reaction relationship between the system and the individual.

The action of conditioning, which is nothing but shackling the individual's mind by the system during extreme situations to detrimental roads of thought, leads the individual to travel only on those roads and suffer the consequences of his or her journey until the human spirit in the person breaks free of the system's stranglehold on its life.

This book narrates the story of one such badly conditioned and weary traveler who used to find solace in darkness every day.

While confronting his conditionings, the first protagonist falls in love with a commercial sex worker, the second protagonist, and in the process, gains enough self-confidence to stand up to those who mistreat him in his milieu.

Darkness begins to give way to light in his life even though he is fired from his job and has to make a fresh beginning with a lower profile job, while at the same time studying for a postgraduate diploma through distance education so that he can find a better job and marry the love of his life.

He succeeds and his life is filled with light.

This book showcases the strength of an unconditional love which succeeds, the fragile power and self-reliance of a woman of the world's oldest profession, the beauty of family structure, and blind kowtowing to power, money, and lust by some educated people and institutions.

Education

is not

Conditioning

But

Liberation

Of Mind

Education is the manifestation of perfection within.

-Swami Vivekananda

Contents

And Then There Was Darkness 15

The Beginning of the Fall 17

Return to Innocence 34

Studies, Exams, and Conditionings 39

Crazy College 41

College for Rudra 45

Decisions after College 50

The Job 52

Dim 70

Unshackled 85

Love 91

And Then There Was Darkness

The boy was born in the dead stillness of the night at two AM. He was the first offspring of his parents who were both the only children of their parents. Thus the birth infused tremendous joy into the modern nuclear family.

Once the happy parents brought their baby home from the maternity hospital, they immediately called an astrologer to their residence to draw their son's horoscope. Their happiness would be short-lived. The astrologer was given the time, date, and place of the boy's birth.

After drawing the baby's horoscope, the astrologer nonchalantly told the new doting parents that their son had been born in *Rahukaalam,* and that he had *Shani Dosha;* astrologers' jargon, commonplace among their clientele, which had pinned a fate upon the infant that he had been born at an inauspicious time and that he would have troubles tormenting him for most of his life.

The cursed infant's mother tightly clutched the loose end of her sari, the *pallu,* and started sobbing heavily into it. The grandparents beat their chests and wailed.

All implored the father of the child to do something. The distraught father turned back to the astrologer to seek a solution. The astrologer threw a life jacket at the father who had been drowning in the ocean of woe. He advised him to name his son 'Rudra,' as it was the name of a *Rigvedic* deity who had been praised as the 'mightiest of the mighty.' The astrologer explained that this would enable his son to fend off the continuous flood of troubles and obstacles that would be flowing rapidly his way for most of his life. This gave some solace to the cursed infant's family. The family had a very holy and grand naming ceremony for their baby. Thus Rudra came to be.

Rudra's baby years were not idyllic. He rarely got a chance to hold toys in his hands. Sacred threads and amulets were tied around his wrists. His parents ferried him from temple to temple, mosque to mosque, church to church, *gurdwara* to *gurdwara*, and one holy place to another. The tender Rudra had to bear the heat of scorching fires which he was made to sit in front of, while holy men fueled the fires by pouring large amounts of pure *ghee* into them as they carried out various kinds of rituals and worship in front of these sacred fires; *yajnas* to save the boy from his fate. The fragile Rudra had to bear the numbing cold of the rushing waters of holy rivers, into which he was dipped naked. He had to succumb to holy ash being rubbed all over him and being brushed roughly with brooms, albeit those made with peacock feathers, by practitioners of the occult. All of this was carried out by his family to ensure a smooth future for Rudra. His nuclear family began to feel a modicum of peace. Time passed and Rudra began to talk intelligibly and walk steadily. He had not been hurt by *life* until this point of time simply because he had been too young, and his family had dealt with his life on his behalf. But now, the tornado of *life* which he had been oblivious to had reached the front doorsteps of his home and the time had come for him to open the front doors and step out to meet what awaited him in the outside world.

The Beginning of the Fall

It was time for Rudra to enter kindergarten to begin his education.

His parents belonged to the upper-middle class, and since he was an only child, they set their sights quite high for their son and chose a wonderful kindergarten, which was one of the best modern ones in the city they lived in. Thus when Rudra entered the kindergarten that had been chosen for him, for the first time, and was left alone with other kids and teachers who were all strangers to him, neither did he burst into tears out of fear nor did he feel awkward and out of place. The kindly smiling teachers, various types of enchanting toys, and walls brightly painted with cartoon characters all held him spellbound. This kindergarten made things easy for the little ones and their parents. All Rudra had to carry from home to kindergarten, and back, with him in his bag suited to his size, was a little notebook, a pencil, an eraser, and a pencil sharpener to help him learn his A, B, Cs. Meanwhile, creative learning tools like coloring books, crayons, and marvelous other goodies including the latest in technology for kids were all provided in the kindergarten itself. This was as good as it got.

Now, life had Rudra in its iron fist, and with the help of conditioning institutions, the first of which would be the kindergarten, and key conditioning persons like teachers, juniors, peers, seniors, and authority figures, including his parents, all who would in one way or another, consciously or unconsciously, affect and damage Rudra, began its game. Rudra was more than a bit of a dreamer. He used to be lost in his own world most of the time. This led to him coming home sans his pencil and eraser, almost every day, having lost them in the fun-filled chaos of the kindergarten. Rudra's parents started becoming more and more frustrated with this carelessness, albeit a childish one of their very own young kid, as days went by. It was not as if they could not afford new pencils and erasers for their only son whom they absolutely adored with intense devotion, but it was the absurdity of the whole situation which caused them increasing frustration.

When their loving and mild admonitions to their son to be more careful with his belongings failed to have any effect on him and the situation remained unchanged, they approached the teachers of the kindergarten and requested them to make sure that their son did not lose his belongings. But, the teachers refused to take that responsibility, and told the parents of the erring child that responsibility could not be spoon-fed, and that they had to teach their son the hard lesson of responsibility the tough way. And when Rudra's parents asked how, the teachers who were veterans at the game of teaching kids lessons, asked them to tie both the pencil and the eraser to their son's wrist every day with long and strong strings when they sent him to the kindergarten, and untie them only when he got back home. They coolly emphasized that this would not only solve the problem but would also teach Rudra a permanent lesson about responsibility. The kid's parents gave a huge sigh and agreed.

The child had to bear the repercussions of this

disciplining action by his elders, however, he could not complain as his carelessness was the cause for it. Rudra could write with his pencil and erase with his eraser, the alphabets and numbers in his notebook easily, but when it came to coloring with crayons and sketch pens in the coloring books, doing other creative activities, and playing with other kids, the pencil and eraser tied to his wrist became a terrible hindrance. He could not even eat from his lunchbox what his mother had lovingly packed for him, without the strings, pencil, and eraser making things incredibly tough for him. The poor child became a butt of jokes for the other kids who delighted in watching him struggle to lead a normal life in spite of the bitter pill of the lesson of responsibility that was being pushed down his throat by his parents and teachers. Now, added to the sacred threads and amulets around his wrists were the strings tied to the pencil and the eraser causing him extreme discomfort at this tender age.

But a day arrived when Rudra could no more bear being tied to his pencil and eraser every day from the time he left for kindergarten until he came back home, and finally begging his parents to free him from his problem, promised to take complete care of his pencil and eraser from that day onwards. That day Rudra's parents sent their son to kindergarten without tying them to his wrist. But he lost them, again. This happened quite a few times after which his parents stopped listening to his woes. Rudra was like a convict with a huge ball of iron shackled to his wrist. The lesson was being drilled into him and he began to grasp it. Was the astrologer's prophecy already starting to come true? Was Rudra really cursed? Was the curse taking hold of him right from this tender age? Was it the curse or was it the milieu? Were Rudra's problems because of the alignment of stars at the time of his birth or simply the makings of his milieu? Were his teachers and parents who had lost trust in him, teaching him responsibility or punishing him? Were they not in the process making him an object of ridicule in the eyes of other kids? Were Rudra's elders not stripping away his self-esteem at an extremely impressionable age?

Rudra was too young to think about these questions. He could only innocently suffer the repercussions of the answers to these questions. Meanwhile, his elders who could and should have thought about these questions were too entangled with the process of running through life without asking why. If only they had slowed down their pace, and maybe even stopped to think for a while, they might have found a better solution to Rudra's conundrum. But it was not to be. Thus, Rudra was conditioned to lose his self-esteem and never ask why at a tender age. Another conditioning was that he had developed a mild, yet unhealthy, fear of being the focus of attention. These conditionings were detrimental consequences at the beginning of his education. Therefore, after kindergarten came to an end, and he was to begin first grade where he would have to wear a uniform, his joy knew no bounds as he thought that he could now quietly merge with the crowd and blend unnoticed into its background. This was a dark thought for such a young age.

Rudra's parents had got admission for their son in a so-called popular school by paying a hefty amount of donation. They had wanted no misfortune to fall upon their young son and had made meticulous preparations. They had bought three complete sets of school uniforms to ensure his comfort. They had also bought four sets of school stationery which included four textbooks for each subject to be taught in the first grade in case their son had not yet completely learnt the lesson of responsibility. Thus, with these multiple armors against loss, and confident that he would go unnoticed among other students on account of all of them wearing identical uniforms, Rudra, on the first day of his first grade, went to his new school in his immaculate new uniform without a single qualm.

The journey to the school on the school bus with other kids was pure joy. But he was cursed. The days at the school used to begin with all the children from various grades assembling in columns, according to their grades, side by side, in the huge ground in front of the main building, and praying together. This prayer used to be led by a student praying into a microphone placed on the platform constructed in front of the main building. After the prayer was over, one of the higher grade students used to read a *'Thought for the Day'* into the microphone. Then another student used to read the school's and general *'News'*. All of this used to be supervised by the principal and senior teachers standing on the platform.

On that first day of school, the first graders were assembled into a column by the teachers, and instructed to pray sincerely and quietly follow the proceedings, and later march to their classroom only when told to and led by a teacher.

The prayer started and Rudra began praying enthusiastically, trying to follow the words. However, during prayer, when everyone was supposed to keep their eyes shut, palms joined, mouth mouthing, and their entire being involved in praying, one mischievous student blew a whistle and threw it away. The whistle landed at

Rudra's feet. Rudra had kept on praying oblivious to this mischievous act, but after the prayer was finished, a teacher whose eyes were supposed to be shut during the prayer but instead whose mind had been, and who had focused only on where the whistle had landed and not who had blown and thrown it away, came down from the platform and approached Rudra. She then picked up the whistle lying at his feet and catching him by his ear dragged him towards the platform. Once the *blind* teacher and the accused student had reached the platform, the *old* teacher made the *new* student kneel down on his knees beside the mike.

Rudra, instead of quietly merging with the crowd and blending into its background, found himself dragged in front of the entire school, and humiliated. His eyes did not brim with tears. They did not even mist. Rudra was in shock. The *'Thought for the Day'* was read. The *'News'* was read. The assembly came to an end. The remaining students dispersed and went to their respective classes.

Rudra was left all alone with the sun beating down upon him. He did not notice the heat of the sun. Neither did he feel the pain in his knees nor the weight of his school bag on his back. Suddenly, Rudra was awakened from his stupor by a hard slap on the back of his head by the teacher who had punished him, and ordered by her to rush to his classroom. He did, but it had been one and a half hours of punishment, and he had missed the very first two classes of his first day in first grade in his new school.

Rudra already had a fear of being the focus of attention. Now it had been strengthened by being humiliated in front of a large crowd. The first day held more disasters for him. Seconds too were served.

Bullies from higher grades came looking for Rudra during lunch break. He was sitting alone at his desk in a corner of his classroom while all the other children had gone out to explore and have lunch outdoors. His lunchbox was in front of him. It was still unopened. Rudra was still feeling utterly miserable. The bullies, after entering the classroom and surrounding their prey's desk, caught hold of Rudra's collar, jerked him to his feet, and threateningly spat on his frightened face that they were there to punish him for the disturbance he had caused that morning in the assembly. They then snatched his lunchbox away from him. After polishing off its contents, the bullies threatened to beat Rudra up if he told any teacher about them or let his parents get even a whiff of the incident, and happily walked away.

Rudra was not afraid of getting beaten up by the bullies. But even after the lunch break, he did not tell any teacher about the bullies snatching his lunch from him and after eating it threatening to beat him up if he told anybody about the incident, for he knew fully well what the teachers would first say to him and what their whole attitude towards him would be. He knew because, when he had come to his classroom after one and a half hours of painful punishment in the sun, on his knees with his schoolbag on his back adding its weight to his humiliation and misery on the platform in front of the whole school, right at the very beginning of his first day in his new school, the very first thing all the teachers who took classes for the first grade till it was time for lunch break had done upon seeing him was to admonish him for his abominable behavior and tell him that he deserved worse punishment for his blasphemy and that he had been fortunate to have been let off so lightly.

Rudra was right. All the teachers who took classes after lunch break too abused Rudra in the same manner as the teachers who had taken classes before lunch break. Rudra suffered silently with a steel claw playing havoc with his insides.

Finally, school hours came to an end, but not his misery. For, while on his way home in the school bus, he was taunted badly by the other kids in such a cruel manner which only kids are capable of. The first day of school ended for Rudra and left him in a daze. No one had spared a thought for the woes of the innocent kid. Rudra reached home physically broken and mentally drained out. His mother had noticed his crestfallen face and defeated demeanor when she had picked him up at the bus stop near their home but had said nothing and had decided to let him do the talking when he himself felt like revealing what had gone wrong in his day. However, Rudra did not want to disappoint his parents. He swallowed the bitter pill of his misery and kept mum about the day's disasters.

After Rudra freshened up, his mother cheerfully announced that his father would be coming home early from work that day, and that she had ordered a large cheese pizza and burgers with fries to celebrate his first day of first grade in his new school. She hoped it would cheer him up.

Rudra forced a smile upon his face and said, "Thank you, dear mother. I am really hungry." The mother was not fooled. Not only was Rudra lying blatantly about his hunger, for he had absolutely no appetite for any kind of food at all, but he also had no appetite for anything at that moment. He endured the long painful wait for his father and the foodstuffs. Rudra had to wait an entire half-hour which seemed like an eternity to him.

Rudra's father came first. Unlike his mother, his father did not notice their son's despair. After hugging Rudra strongly and kissing him fondly on both cheeks, his father said, "I bet you had a great first day at your new school. Let's celebrate this occasion. The delicacies you love will be arriving at any moment. I am famished." He then went to freshen up. By the time Rudra's father came back, the pizza and the burgers with fries, all piping hot, had arrived.

As all of them sat down together to eat, Rudra's mother was cautious enough not to probe into her son's day at school, but soon his father, taking hold of a large slice of pizza after wolfing down a few fries, cheerfully asked Rudra, "So, what was special at school today son?"

Rudra quietly replied, "Everything was great, father. "He was again lying through his teeth, but he made his father happy. His mother's heart gave a twinge. But she kept quiet. Rudra, in order to keep up appearances, forced down two slices of pizza and a burger down his throat. It was pure torture. He did not touch any fries which were his favorite but left his share to his father who loved them more than his son.

Once the feast was over, the head of the family announced, "Let's watch cartoons," and turning on the television, plumped down on the sofa. Rudra and his mother were expected to join him, and they did. When Rudra's mother sat down next to her son on the sofa, she suddenly noticed his knees. Rudra was a fair boy, and they had turned a little purple due to his punishment in the morning. Rudra's mother could not contain herself anymore. She threw her arms around her son tightly and in a pleading manner said softly, "Son, please tell us what's wrong. I promise you that we will find a solution to your problem. After all, we are your parents." Rudra replied in a low voice, "Please let me go to sleep. I am very tired." Before his mother could say anything, his father said in a gentle tone, "It is ok son. You don't have to tell us anything right now. Take your time. But remember, you are a big boy now. Be brave. Go and sleep." Rudra's mother released her son from her hug and he immediately ran to his bedroom.

Rudra shut the door, drew the curtains across the windows tightly, turned off all the lights, jumped into bed, and drawing a thick blanket over his entire body including his head, lay in the dark, blocking out all thoughts to escape being traumatized by them.

Darkness suddenly became his mighty fortress. It was a place where he was safe and where only he existed. The rest of the world was kept at bay. In the darkness, all his troubles seemed so far away. This would be his permanent cure for the worldly travails he had to endure, and also a source of great solace. But now the question arises as to really why Rudra had not protested his innocence.

The answer was not only simple but also deep and terrible. Since he had a deep-rooted fear of being the focus of attention and could easily lose his self-esteem at the snap of a finger, and that too without a reason, his mind had become completely blank when he had been suddenly targeted amidst the gathering of the entire school because of something which he was not even remotely guilty of. He had become numb and allowed circumstances to have their way with him. And the circumstances had not been gentle.

This action in a strong conditioning institution at the

beginning of his life a school with its teachers and other students had strengthened what conditioning had already happened in kindergarten. Rudra's mild fear of being the focus of attention had escalated into a terror at being so in the midst of a crowd. He felt that only humiliation and misery lay at being the focus of attention and found solace in the darkness of loneliness which he considered solitude.

Despite Rudra's tribulations during the day, he was still a kid, and soon fell asleep aided by the darkness which acted as a fortress against the thoughts revolving around his travails of the day. And, when he woke up the next morning, he was still a kid, and some bruises had healed, like the one where the bullies had eaten his lunch and threatened to beat him up if he let anyone come to know about their dastardly act. Also, all the wicked taunts by the kids on the school bus while returning home. But the conditionings held firm in his sub-consciousness.

So, on the second day, Rudra was neither wildly enthusiastic about going to school nor was he rigidly reluctant. He calmly went about getting ready for school and his parents let him be and did not broach the topic of the previous day. His mother packed his lunch and walked him to the bus stop. Fortunately for the young boy, only a few kids held on to what had happened to him the day before, and did not find many partners to abuse him into oblivion. Hence, Rudra was spared the taunts and had a comfortable journey to school.

However, the bullies did not spare him that day at lunch break. They again hijacked Rudra's lunch on his second day in school. But no other misfortune befell him, as miraculously, even all the teachers spared him their cutting remarks. The same happened for the next four days until the week ended on a Sunday. Rudra had succeeded in wearing a grey suit, not standing out from the crowd, and being indistinguishable from the rest, as far as anybody else except the bullies were concerned. Maybe, it was not entirely the bullies' fault, because Rudra's mother was such an excellent cook, and Rudra was such an innocent and easy prey, that predators would be tempted beyond reasonable bounds to satisfy their appetite for a prey. And, as for the tormented Rudra, complete darkness at the end of the day was his only solace. It became a habit.

Finally, beginning from the first Monday of the second week of school, Rudra started having a heavy breakfast at home before going to school, and stopped taking his lunchbox with him, for the rest of his school days. When his mother initially asked why, he obfuscated the matter by simply stating that he did not like eating cold food, and his mother quietly accepted his explanation. And, as far as the bullies with their threats were concerned, they proved to be only bluster, and were left frustrated at the absence of Rudra's lunchbox with him. After these initial tumultuous incidents, Rudra finally sailed through the rest of his days in first grade, and passing its exams, he moved on to the second grade. He quietly went about his studies and managed to keep a low profile in the second grade until one day when the curse reared its ugly head again.

That fateful day, Rudra forgot to pack in his schoolbag the textbook for one of the subjects that were to be taught that day. And, when that particular class started in school, and the teacher found out that Rudra had not brought his textbook, she screamed at him and made him stand up on the bench with his arms raised above his head for the entire duration of the class. Rudra, who had carefully avoided being the center of attention for a long time, was again devastated at being so. Another conditioning took place.

Rudra became deathly afraid of making even the smallest of mistakes, terrified that they would invoke the wrath of authority. This led to a bizarre behavior by him from the next day onwards. That morning, while getting ready for school, Rudra begged his mother to come and sit beside him while he packed his school bag for the day. He then placed the day's school timetable where both of them could see it and asked her to watch and make sure that he packed in his schoolbag every one of the textbooks for all the subjects that were to be taught that day in school. Rudra painfully dragged out the process by placing the first textbook, for the first class to be taken in school according to the timetable for that day, in his schoolbag, then immediately brought it out partly to make sure it was the right one, and kept on repeating the process until his exasperated mother reassured him that he had got it right and told him that he should move on to placing the next textbook in the bag. Each and every textbook required for the day underwent this obsessive-compulsive paranoid treatment. At the end of the ordeal of "helping" Rudra pack his schoolbag, his mother was at her wits' end, while her son who had been a bundle of nerves before was just completely drained out. This terrible ordeal occurred for both every single school day until Rudra completed third grade. At the beginning of fourth grade, Rudra's mother, who had to put an end to this insane ritual, finally firmly told him that getting punished now and then by teachers was better than punishing himself every day. She hoped that since Rudra was now slightly grown up, this line of reasoning would make sense to him. It did.

Rudra gave up his nerve-wracking behavior in the mornings and started packing his schoolbag by himself without getting paranoid or obsessively compulsive about it. It was not easy to digest overnight, but his mother was firm about her decision, and Rudra had no other option. But, sometimes, when his withdrawal symptoms from his paranoia and obsessive- compulsive behavior got too hard to handle, he scratched and dragged the nails of his hands down the walls which were whitewashed, out of the sight of his parents.

The conditionings were really taking a heavy toll on him. However, deathly darkness had been his solace before and it comforted him even more now. Rudra grew up. He studied very hard and extremely well. But he never excelled in exams. However, his parents were happy with his performances in the exams, and never pressurized him to do more than what he was already doing.

Rudra had friends, but not close ones, and he didn't belong to any group. He had casual friends. He played games with others but was not a good team player. And he was not good at sports played by individuals. Thus, he was not in any of the sports teams of the school. His conditionings left no room for him to be in any sort of cultural activities. Outside of school too, Rudra had just casual friends in his neighborhood, and school with its necessary studies left little time for him to socialize with them. And that was that. Going by Pink Floyd, on the outside, Rudra was just, "Another brick in the wall." However, he had his personal conditionings, and soon entered high school bearing their heavy burden in his young heart.

Now, Rudra was no longer a kid. He had grown up and there were quite a few beautiful girls in the school. He could not help but noticing them and taking furtive glances at them whenever they were around him. And that was the beginning and end of his activities concerning girls.

But the same could not be said of other boys. There was one exquisite pearl of a girl in Rudra's class. While Rudra was satisfied with taking a look at her in a furtive manner a few times during the day, a few other boys in his class were not. One of the lover boys, who was a budding writer, had filled two full pages of one of his homework books about how he would shower his love on her, and another, who was his brother from another mother, had bought an 'I Love You' greeting card, and had filled it up with her name.

Meanwhile, another boy who had realized the importance of money, and was of the view that beauty follows wealth, had started buying lottery tickets sold outside the school compound, going against the rules of the school. And, as is the norm where there is something fascinating cooking against the rules set by the authorities, there is always somebody who becomes a snitch; usually a person who is a nobody.

All the mischievous deeds of the three notorious boys were common knowledge among the backbenchers, and upon the information provided by the snitch who was also a backbencher, there was a raid on the class by senior teachers. They immediately caught hold of the erring students, and upon searching their bags and pockets, found the homework book with the elaborate writings on love, the 'I Love You' greeting card, and the lottery tickets.

When the three backbenchers were about to be hauled away from class for punishment, the student who aspired to get rich quickly came up with the ingenious idea that it would help to have someone who had a better reputation than them with them, so that the punishment would become less severe. He knew that Rudra took furtive looks at the girl and that he would meekly surrender to the authorities. Hence, he told the teachers hauling him away by his collar that even Rudra was involved in the affair involving the beautiful girl in their class. The teachers wanted to prove a point and caught hold of Rudra too without any proof. They made the four boys stand outside the teachers' staffroom in a line and calmly told them that they would enter their names in the 'Black Book.' The teachers also sternly told the boys that they would inform their parents about them breaking the school's rules with their disgusting deeds.

All four students gave a shiver. It was well known in the school that if your name was entered in the 'Black Book,' you would be rusticated from the school if you committed even the smallest of offences after that. Everybody had heard of the 'Black Book' as being a menacing black leather-bound huge book which horrified those whose names were to be written in it. Only a few got to see it, and those who did never spoke of it.

One of the teachers went into the staffroom and brought out a small, thin, and worn-out book with a brown cover. Even in such a dire situation, Rudra learnt a valuable lesson which was 'Don't judge a book by its cover.'

When the teacher opened the book and took out his pen, Rudra broke down completely. He begged his teachers not to put his name in the "Black Book" nor inform his parents about something he had not done. The teachers who were only interested in the why and the how now suddenly had to deal with the who. They did not know Rudra or his name, for he was the boy in grey. But they knew the other three boys and their names. This softened them a bit. Copious tears started flowing down Rudra's cheeks. The three notorious students imitated Rudra skillfully. There was a lot of loud pleading and wailing by the four students. The teachers' hearts softened more.

All because of Rudra as they realized that they had nothing against the boy, except the statement made by one of his notorious classmates who had been caught red-handed. The lottery ticket buyer had been clever. In unity lies strength, and now that the three culprits stood united with Rudra, they had a good chance of escaping with a light punishment. And escape with light punishment they did. For, the teachers felt that they should treat all the students equally, and because they could not punish Rudra severely, they would give all one more chance to improve themselves. They agreed not to inform the boys' parents or write their names in the 'Black Book' provided they changed their characters for the better and behaved like students instead of casanovas and gamblers. But there was punishment.

All four had to kneel down in the middle of the school ground with their arms raised above their heads for an entire day under the sun. Rudra had come full circle. The conditioning that Rudra got imprinted with was that looking at nubile females was a crime which resulted in one losing one's character. Again darkness stood by his side. Time flowed.

Return to Innocence

Now, coming to Rudra's life outside of kindergarten and school, it could not be said that that it was ordinary. But, barring a few incidents, it was definitely not unique, and was in fact quite quiet, simple, and stuck to the basics. As a baby, Rudra had been calm most of the time and had not cried much. He had been fed whenever he had to be fed.

When Rudra had learnt to walk, he had done so within the boundaries set by his parents.

He had been a mild child and had not exceeded limits. Rudra had never indulged in throwing and breaking toys. He had handled his possessions gently. This had all been due to the love and care with which Rudra's parents had brought him up. But, there were a few qualities in him which his parents did not know where they came from, and thus astounded them.

Rudra ate in moderation. He was not fussy about the food he was given to eat and always finished the food on his plate. Rudra loved toys, chocolates, and ice creams. But he never pestered his parents for them, especially when they went out to have a good time.

When Rudra began attending birthday parties of kids whose parents knew his parents, he never asked his parents for new clothes to wear to the birthday parties or for them to hold his birthday party at home and celebrate it by inviting other kids. He was not only content with the clothes he had but was also satisfied with the little socializing he did at those birthday parties and whatever interaction he had with other kids in the park where his mother took him to play during the evenings.

Rudra was a very innocent child. Being low key, he only had casual friends. But he was contented with himself. Thus Rudra was the jewel of this nuclear family,even with all his debilitating conditionings.

All these behavioral traits showed Rudra in a good light. However, the first problem his parents had encountered in raising their son was when they had to tie a pencil and an eraser to his wrist with long and strong strings after he had begun to lose his belongings. Rudra had complained vehemently for the first time in his life. His parents had tried to avoid their son's pain by stopping what to the three in the nuclear family had been pure torture, but circumstances had dictated otherwise, and they had gone ahead with what they had considered to be inhuman behavior. This episode had pained Rudra's parents greatly.

Rudra had withdrawn a little into a shell. But he had been just a very young kid and darkness had not yet become his staunch friend. Fortunately, by the end of kindergarten, Rudra had learnt his lesson. His parents had been jubilant and had hoped that his new beginning in first grade in a new school would not only cheer him up but also infuse him with greater enthusiasm for life. They had spent a huge amount of money on his admission to the new school. The school was the best in their city and was also well known in the surrounding towns and cities. To be short, it was 'Popular.'

Rudra's parents had made elaborate preparations for their son's next step in education. But disaster had struck the very first day. The morning had been full of cheer when Rudra had started off to school. But when he had come home, looking like a broken warrior, and would say nothing of the events during his first day in the new school, and had also evaded questions as to whether some misfortune had befallen him, his mother had become uneasy, but not unduly worried. However, later when she had seen Rudra's tender knees which had turned purple due to his punishment that first day in first grade in his new school, and he still would not explain what had happened, her soul had wept, and only her husband's strong will and smart actions had prevented her from crying in front of her already beleaguered son. The second problem which had cropped up, one which his parents had not expected even in their wildest dreams was Rudra's infatuation with darkness.

Rudra used to study and do his homework well, when he came back from school. But after twilight, when he had spare time, instead of watching television or spending quality time with his parents, he used to spend it in his dark bedroom. Rudra had no hobbies, and only rarely went out to play with his casual friends. He refused to meet guests who came to his home and lay in his niche of darkness.

Rudra's parents had become really worried and had consulted their family doctor. The good doctor had said that these things happen to sensitive children and had asked them to go to their son's school without his knowledge and find out what had exactly happened there so that the cause for Rudra's abnormal behavior could be pinpointed. And when Rudra's parents had gone to his school, and had met the principal, all that they had received was a heap of abuse against their son's character and what he had done to deserve his punishment. However, Rudra's parents had not believed even a single word that had come out of the principal's mouth, and had gone back to their family doctor with the details. After the doctor had listened to them, he had sighed deeply and had said that unfortunately, it was the case for a psychiatrist and not for a physician like him. But the good doctor had also told Rudra's parents that their son was still very young and that they better spare him the psychiatrist's pills and try to solve the matter at home with lots of love and affection. Rudra's parents' views had matched that of their family doctor's. They had begun to give more love and attention to their son at home to bolster his self-confidence.

Whenever there had been school holidays, Rudra's parents had taken him to various places of interest within and outside the city. His young mind had begun to expand as a result of visiting museums and places of historical significance. They had gone and stayed in nature resorts. There they had gone on nature walks. Rudra had started enjoying life along with his happy parents. He had especially found joy in the simple things of life, like feeling the petals of a wildflower in all their softness between his fingers without plucking the blossom. Normalcy had begun to enter Rudra's life. But misery had not been far away.

As second grade had been nearing its end, Rudra had made a tiny mistake of not bringing to school, the textbook of one of the subjects to be taught that day. He had been punished, and he had simply freaked out. This time, the way he , day after day, made his mother verify that he had perfectly packed his school bag for the day, went beyond sane norms. The time had come for a psychiatrist. Rudra's parents had wanted to spare their son the further agony of letting him know that his behavior was abnormal. Thus, they had visited a popular psychiatrist without their son's knowledge, and had explained his symptoms to the specialist doctor. After the psychiatrist had listened to Rudra's parents patiently, the specialist in mental health had written a prescription, and had asked them to powder the pills, mix it in food, and give it to their son. This, Rudra's parents had begun to do regularly. But he had been conditioned beyond repair. When things had not improved with Rudra, at every visit of his parents, the psychiatrist had started to change drugs and increase the dosage.

Finally, a time had come when Rudra was being given drugs equivalent to those which were given to the inmates of a lunatic asylum. But there had been no improvement in his behavior. Actually, it had worsened. Rudra's mother had simply been unable to bear it anymore. She had asked the psychiatrist to taper off the drugs that were being given to her son and finally stop them altogether. The psychiatrist had been glad to wash his hands off the crazy kid.

Once Rudra had been taken off psychiatric drugs, his mother had made a simple statement that getting punished now and then by teachers was better than punishing himself every day. This had made Rudra stop his paranoid and obsessive-compulsive schoolbag packing behavior. But now and then, he had begun to give vent to his frustrations by scratching and dragging the nails of his fingers down the walls which were whitewashed, out of sight of his parents. This had been the jetsam and flotsam of Rudra's encounter with the psychiatrist and his drugs.

Studies, Exams, and Conditionings

As far as the studies were concerned, Rudra studied very hard and understood subjects extremely well. But when exams came, he did not excel in them. The reason for his failure to deliver was the conditioning of his psyche by the obsessive-compulsive disorder.

Rudra, even though he mastered subjects thoroughly before the exams, during them due to his obsessive-compulsive disorder, checked over and over again whether the answer he had written in his answer paper to a question in the question paper was perfect before he moved on to answering the next question, and therefore always running out of time in answering all the questions in the question papers, failed to turn his excellent knowledge into good marks. His obsessive-compulsive disorder during examinations got worse as he moved up from one grade to the next and his pressure on himself escalated. The number of times Rudra checked for the perfection of an answer he had written to a question before he moved on to answering the next question in the question paper started escalating as he moved towards the twelfth grade. Thus, when he appeared for twelfth-grade examinations, Rudra's parents had already prepared for the worst. But they were tremendously relieved when the results were announced. Rudra had somehow managed to clear his twelfth-grade examinations. Therefore, taking all factors into consideration, Rudra's parents decided to make it easy on his psyche from then on and guided him towards an education where not only would his mind be not taxed much during it, but which would also later help him to take on a simple profession; one which would not ruffle his sensibilities, and that too provided he chose to work.

Rudra's parents were well aware of the competitive world and had saved enough for their son to lead a comfortable life without him having to slog at a job in a dog eat dog life. All they wanted was to enable him to handle the money they had saved for him cautiously, enough to last him till the end of his life. Not only his life but also the life of the family he would eventually have. They got him enrolled in a Commerce College. Life is competitive. There is competition not only for wealth but even for basic survival. And for basic survival, not only money is needed, but more importantly, a strong family structure is essential. For a strong family structure provides one with the immaculate mental framework and monetary support necessary for basic survival in a disordered negative world. And Rudra's psyche was fragile because of the disordered negative world. Hence, foremost of all, he had the necessity of a strong family structure. Thankfully he had it.

Crazy College

Rudra's parents had once more spared no effort or money in getting their son admitted to a very popular educational institution; this time a college. Now, there is a difference between the terms prestigious and popular. What is prestigious is certainly popular, but what is popular may not necessarily be prestigious. But in modern times, especially in big cities, the terms prestigious and popular are confused with one another, and most often are taken to mean the same. And since Rudra's parents had spent loads of money and effort in getting their son admitted to that particular popular college, in their eyes that college was prestigious.

The college was popular for a reason. Not only the highly intelligent students who had scored extremely well in twelfth-grade examinations sought admission there to avail of its excellent up-to-date infrastructure, but also the children of the high society people jostled there for admissions, even those with poor twelfth-grade marks because the college had a reputation for giving almost complete freedom to the students in the way they attended classes, completed their assignments and projects, and finally how and when they decided to take the final exams and graduate from the college. It was too good to be true. But it was true.

Now, generally, college after twelfth grade is like letting loose a mischievous monkey from its cage. You are eighteen years of age. Your blood is hot. Your hormones are pumping. You are free from the straitjacket of a uniform. You can wear torn jeans, tight tee shirts, tops with rebellious slogans, miniskirts, and whatnot. You can crop your hair to look almost bald, leave it quite long, or let it dangle somewhere between the two extremities; something which applies for all sexes. You are eligible to drive. Depending on your parents' finances, you can have a bike or a car of your own, or if you have one or more than one already, you can legally enjoy the drive with friends. Further, again depending on your parents' finances, you can hang out at cafes with your buddies as there is more free time, with your parents' trust in you to spend both their money and your time harmlessly.

Going even further, once again depending on your parents' finances, if you are a young lady, you can use the perfect makeup kit to match the color of the makeup of your eyes and lips with the color of one of your numerous purses, dresses, and footwear, so that all will match and accentuate your look when you blush, while if you are a young gentleman, you can afford to date such a young lady. There will be good moments. There will be bad episodes. New friends will be made. Old ones will drift away. Old groups will be exited as the feeling that the air has become stale and the atmosphere is becoming suffocating, becomes overpowering. New groups will be joined to enjoy a breath of fresh air. Love will come. Love will go. Breakups are healed by time and friends. Exams will come. One will fare well, okay, or poorly. But someday almost all will certainly graduate. The college was all set to begin. It was ready for its fresh batch of first semester students. Rudra too was waiting to start. In fact, he was raring to go.

Rudra was tired of his school and also the kindergarten

in his faraway past, which he vividly remembered even though twelve years had passed, and the agonies both had caused him. He had heard about the freedom the college offered and was anticipating his tryst with destiny. Unfortunately, Rudra the young man did not realize at this point in time that the agonies that had been caused to him in school and kindergarten were not burdens that could be left behind in a particular place or time but instead were products of the conditionings of the mind. And that, if he wanted to be free of agony, and begin his efforts towards keeping his tryst with whatever was his destiny, he had to first free his mind from its conditionings and become its master instead of remaining its servant. If Rudra thought that freedom lay at the top of a mountain where the college perched and at the base of which rested the kindergarten and school and that he could by climbing the mountain to reach the college leaving behind the school and kindergarten, be free, he was completely mistaken. Because, unfortunately, he would be bringing his conditioned mind with him from the bottom of the mountain, and he would not be free even at its top. His agonies would still haunt him at the top of the mountain even after he had made the laborious effort of climbing it. But Rudra was oblivious to this, and therefore happy. His parents too were on the same track as their son.

Rudra's father told him that he wanted to buy a macho motorcycle for him now that his son had become a man. But here is where the conditionings subtly played their devious games. Rudra smilingly declined his father's offer of a costly macho motorcycle, and instead opted for a cheap fuel efficient moped. The conditionings were not yet done with the young man. When his parents took him shopping for new clothes and footwear, Rudra did not opt for costly branded clothes and shoes but instead settled for cheap simple clothes and sandals. As a last measure, his father tried to make his son buy a hip jacket. The result was the same. Rudra said a strong, "No," to the stylish jacket. He instead bought a simple sleeveless sweater for the cold times. All this left his parents in confusion. On the day all three had gone shopping, after the simple purchases, they went for dinner in a well-known restaurant. After having ordered starters, under a relaxed and luxurious ambience, Rudra's father asked him:

"What is the matter, son? Why are you refusing the good things of life? You know we can afford them. Come on, talk to me; man to man."

His mother pleaded:

"Open up dear. Feel free to share anything with us. After all, we are your parents."

Rudra smiled softly at both and replied:

"There is nothing wrong mother. Actually, I am very happy, father. Both of you need not worry about me. I wanted to tell both of you before, but never found the time for it. Now is the perfect moment. I believe that I am a changed personality now that I have finished my twelfth grade and am about to enter college. I am feeling very enthusiastic about it. Only my tastes are simple. That's all. There is absolutely nothing to worry about."

Rudra was happy. His parents were satisfied with his answers and they too became cheerful. Everybody enjoyed the dinner. Rudra had said "There is absolutely nothing to worry about." Nothing could have been further from the truth.

College for Rudra

The first day of college finally arrived. Rudra got up early, freshened up cheerfully, and got ready meticulously. The cup of his expectations was brimming dangerously. He was wearing new clothes and was carrying books, calculator, laptop, and whatnot in his new backpack.

Before Rudra took his first step towards his tryst with his destiny, his mother performed the ritual of *Aarti* by lighting a lamp and blessing him with its holy flame. She then applied a *Tilak* on her son's forehead using vermillion. Both the *Aarti* and the *Tilak*, the mother hoped, would ensure that her son was blessed by the gods.

When Rudra slipped on his new sandals and came out of the front door, his father was waiting beside Rudra's new moped. Rudra's father himself had washed the moped thoroughly and had performed its *Puja* by breaking a coconut near its front wheel and also draping its headlight with a garland. He hugged his son and both the parents wished Rudra a great first day in college after which the young man left home on his moped. Rudra's parents wanted an auspicious start to their son's future. They would leave no stone unturned in the effort.

But other forces greater than their efforts were at play too. These forces were the forces of fate. It is fate that has the final word. And it was fate that was waiting for Rudra in the parking area of the college.

Now, the college authorities were so conscientious as a result of knowing that they had fleeced their students' parents as best as they could, that they provided the best infrastructure for their students. For example, even the parking area for the students was so posh, that the senior rich students hung out there with their fancy vehicles and girlfriends or boyfriends. It was considered prestigious to be let into the groups which haunted the parking area and join them in smoking cigarettes and just being hip.

On the first day of college, these members of the parking area club had arrived early and were waiting for the new students of the college to arrive in their den so that they could rag them. Rudra came early to the college and was the first new student to arrive in the parking area in all his enthusiasm. The pride of male lions and lionesses was waiting. Finally, a prey had come close to the grasp of the predators. It was a fawn. As in the wild, since the prey was small and weak, the male lions took no part in hunting and allowed the lionesses the pleasure of the hunt and the kill. The males would only enjoy the view and the feast.

As the senior girl students in their skimpy and tight clothes ragged him, Rudra, who could not even take a good look at them due to his conditioning, was left aghast, and also suffocated by the cigarette smoke of the senior girls who were doing the ragging and their boyfriends who were watching. Involuntarily, his eyes closed tightly as he started shivering and broke into a cold sweat within just a few minutes of ragging. Seeing this, the senior students became worried that Rudra was going into some kind of seizure or shock, and stopping the ragging, ordered him to leave the premises of their club. The hunt was over as soon as it had started.

The fun was cut short as the prey had not allowed the predators the pleasure of a good kill. Rudra literally ran away from the parking area. It may have seemed to the onlookers that the fawn had survived the mighty pride of lions and lionesses because of its fragility. But severe damage had been done. A dream had been shattered.

Rudra barely made it through the first day's classes sanely. It had been a merry day of introductions and interactions with classmates and teachers. But Rudra had not enjoyed it even one bit and had just sleepwalked through everything. Finally, it was time for the first day of college to end and the students to go home. Quaking with fear, Rudra approached the parking area. Fortunately for him, it was filled with all manner of students taking out their vehicles. He too pulled out his moped from its parking spot and quickly made his way home.

Now, Rudra was not a good actor, as his history proved the same. He could hide his disappointment. But he could not put on a cheerful demeanor. Therefore, when he reached home, his parents noticed that something wrong had come to the fore once more, and simply went about greeting their son with lots of unconditional love and tried to cheer him up as best as they could without probing into his first day at college. But Rudra ate little and went early to bed in his bedroom with all its darkness. The family's hearts which had held joy in the morning had now been emptied of that wonderful emotion and filled with grief instead.

The next day, Rudra, after entering the college campus, went to park his moped in the parking area with great trepidation. But he need not have worried, for he was conditioned to lose his self-esteem and never ask why at a tender age and the gang lords of the parking area simply threw taunts at him and did nothing else. However, this was not the end of it. And he was not conditioned for what would come. Instead, it would condition him for the future.

The senior girls who had ragged Rudra in the parking area spread the word around the campus that Rudra was an easy target for some wicked fun. Many other senior girls, and even more than a few girls who were his classmates, began to taunt Rudra whenever and wherever they got the chance. The laughter of the boys who watched the humiliation of Rudra encouraged these girls to go even further and the taunts started becoming lewd.

The first semester was sheer hell for Rudra. He had gone back to black every time he could, to escape from his misery. He simply could not concentrate on his studies. Rudra barely passed all the subjects of the first semester.

Luckily for Rudra after the first semester ended and the second semester started, the people who used to make his life miserable simply lost interest in taunting him. It was because Rudra had absorbed every single taunt like a sponge absorbs water and had not shown even a little bitof anger at the humiliation piled upon him. Added to this, the teachers of the college who had been witnesses to these taunts had not interfered and simply dismissed them as fair game between grown-up students. To taunt Rudra further without him revolting or the authorities reacting would be simply boring for those who enjoyed tormenting. Therefore, the students who had proved to be a terror for Rudra moved on without giving a single thought to what they had done.

But the relief that Rudra felt after the first semester was over and the other students left him to himself was beyond measure. It was as if his small fishing boat had survived a storm in the middle of an ocean. At home, his parents noticed the change, and they too heaved a sigh of relief. Rudra could finally concentrate on his studies.

The teachers had been insensitive, and they still were. It was alright. They did not matter. They had neither taunted Rudra nor enjoyed the humiliation he had gone through. Rudra moved on without worrying about anybody or what had transpired, studied hard, and graduated from college with a first-class degree.But what had happened in the first six months of college had scarred and conditioned him beyond measure.

Decisions after College

Rudra had graduated from college with decent marks despite his life-shattering conditionings. He had been conditioned to easily lose his self-esteem and never ask why. He had been conditioned to fear being the focus of attention, and this dread increased exponentially with respect to the number of people around him. He had been conditioned to have a morbid fear of making even the smallest of mistakes that would invoke the wrath of authority. He had been conditioned to think unnaturally that looking at nubile females was a crime which resulted in one losing one's character. Furthermore, he had obsessive-compulsive disorder, which escalated with fear and mangled his senses.

It was a miracle that Rudra had come so far in his schooling and procured a first-class degree. Rudra's parents thought that he had suffered enough of schooling and that it would now be good for him to settle down in a low-key job that would not demand much effort from him, and where he would be content and happy for the rest of his life; a quiet job for him only if he wished to be employed.

He too had had enough of studying and agreed with his parents; expressing his desire to work and keep busy.So, the doting couple used their influential connections and got their cherished son a job as an assistant to a deputy manager of a bank in a nearby metropolis. Since their family was a nuclear family, all that the parents had earned and saved was for their son, and it was quite a large sum.

It would not have mattered to them if Rudra did not want to work at all, taking into consideration his conditionings. Therefore, the middle-aged parents were least bothered about the position or salary in their grown-up son's job. This had led to their string-pulling without considering its after-effects. As for Rudra, he was a simple guy. His needs were less, ego was small. As a result, he too did not care about his salary or position in his first job.

Rudra's parents rented a neat house for him in the metropolis where he was to work, furnished it well, and despite his vehement protests, bought a snazzy new car for him. They knew that they could not be there forever for him, and therefore decided not to shift their place of residence from the city to the metropolis; an inaction which would enable their only son to get adjusted to being alone, at least until the time when he got married and had a family of his own.

It was now Rudra alone, versus the entire world.

The Job

The house that Rudra's parents had rented for him was in a quiet and posh residential locality of the metropolis. Just at a brisk fifteen minutes' walk from his new home was an excellent vegetarian restaurant where he could have his breakfast and dinner on working days, and also his lunch on holidays. Beside the restaurant was a shopping mall that catered to the myriad needs of the consumers. Rudra's parents had thought of everything, or so it seemed.

Rudra barely had time to get acclimatized to the metropolis before the day arrived when he had to report for work. He turned on Google Maps on his iPhone and began driving. He had heard about the many-headed monster that traffic in this metropolis was, and since he hadn't wanted to be even a minute late on his very first day at his first job, he had left his home quite early.

Breakfast had been forgotten as there had been a huge swarm of butterflies fluttering in his stomach. As Rudra drove through the maddening traffic, his nerves were constantly on the edge. Finally, when he reached the bank and parked his car, he found that he was one hour early. The bank's doors were closed. Rudra's nerves were still jittery. The reason for his discomfort was not the nerve-wracking drive through the crazy traffic. It was homemade.

Rudra had landed his job without giving an interview

or through any formal recruitment process of the bank. His father had known the deputy manager of the bank, and luckily, when he had asked the deputy manager if there was any way in which he could help his son Rudra to get a job, the post of assistant to the deputy manager had been vacant, and the deputy manager had immediately told Rudra's father that he would be happy to hire his son as his assistant.

Rudra had never taken anybody's favor until this point in time. Now he had taken a favor. And the favor was not a small one, but quite a big one. It not only flouted the norms but was also completely illegal. Rudra's self-esteem was under the scanner once more. He would certainly be the focus of attention in his new workplace. And he would have to work under authority making doubly sure that he did not commit even a single tiny mistake. His devils had come back to haunt him. To be realistic, they had never left him.

Rudra had worried, and now kept on worrying, about how he would fare in his first job on the very first day, until the security guard unlocked the doors of the bank and opened them. Customers had already gathered in front of the bank by then. They jostled with one another to get inside. After the small crowd had entered the bank, and the way was clear, Rudra made his way into his new workplace. He took out his phone and dialed the number of deputy manager.The phone on the other side rang. There was no answer. Rudra tried two more times.

The deputy manager's phone kept on ringing at each try, but he didn't take the call.

Rudra got flustered. Then, the new employee, after locating a cabin displaying 'Deputy Manager' boldly on a board on its door, gathered enough courage and knocked. There came a voice from the inside, "Come in." Rudra trembled as he pushed open the door and entered the deputy manager's cabin.

The deputy manager asked him in a gruff voice:

"Who are you? What do you want?"

When Rudra replied as to who he was, the deputy manager asked him angrily:

"Why are you so late? And was it you who was calling me on my mobile and disturbing me when the morning's hectic work has already started?"

Rudra's heartbeat and pulse rate increased as he tremblingly replied:

"But sir, I had come one hour early. The security guard opened the doors just a few minutes ago."

The deputy manager's anger increased even further as he said:

"There is a separate entrance for employees of the bank. We have to come one hour early to prepare for the entire day's work. What prevented you from calling me beforehand and getting to know about how this bank functions? By the way, how did you come to the bank from your home?"

Rudra's sweat had made his shirt wet as he replied:

"In my car, sir."

The deputy manager asked:

"Which brand and model of car? Is it new?"

Rudra gave the details asked by his boss about the

vehicle his father had bought for him.

The deputy manager's voice took on a sarcastic tone as he asked:

"You want everything easily in life, don't you? Just like this job, right? By the way, how many bottles of perfume have you poured on yourself?"

Rudra tried to stutter out a reply but could not.

The deputy manager suddenly calmed down and said:

"Look boy this is the metropolis. Get smart fast. If you exhibit your money along with your innocence, people will eat you alive. Anyway, coming back to your work, do what my computer operator tells you for a few days until you get your sea legs. You can call me Mr. Khanna and my computer operator's name is Raveena. I expect only the best from you as I have a high regard for your father. That was the reason for my earlier show of anger.

Now get going. Money has to be made."

Rudra, while wiping the perspiration from his face, said:

"Thank you very much, Mr. Khanna," and left.

After exiting the deputy manager's cabin, Rudra went to the enquiry counter and asked where he could find the deputy manager's computer operator. The woman manning the enquiry counter simply lifted her hand and pointed her finger at a young woman about Rudra's age who was working on a computer in a glass cubicle. Rudra said, "Thank you," and gathering all his confidence, approached the computer operator whose name was Raveena.

He said in a low voice, "Good morning Ms. Raveena."

Without taking her eyes off the computer screen, Raveena exploded, "It is Mrs. Nayak for whoever you are." She then simply went on with her work.

It was as if Rudra had been hit by lightening. But it was simply conditioning. However, he managed to squeeze out a weak, "Please excuse me, Mrs. Nayak," from his vocal cords. This time the young woman looked at him and sighing deeply, asked:

"Alright, who are you? What do you want? You can see that I am extremely busy. Please make your business short."

Rudra, who was feeling dizzy, somehow managed to answer:

"Mrs. Nayak, my name is Rudra Suryavanshi. I am the new assistant to the deputy manager."

He then took a deep breath. But the pause was too long for Mrs. Nayak and she again burst out:

"So what should I do? Go away and stop disturbing me."

Rudra started quaking badly, but he managed to squeak:

"But please Mrs. Nayak, Mr. Khanna told me that you would tell me what to do."

Mrs. Nayak shifted her eyes from him back onto the computer screen and simply said:

"Well, he didn't tell me anything. Don't disturb me anymore. Go away Rudra."

Rudra was not addressed as Mr. Suryavanshi. The young woman had reduced his status to the status of an office boy. Rudra didn't know what to do, where to sit, or whom to ask for help. He simply stood by the water cooler the whole day watching the customers and other employees of the bank busy with their lives. It was as if he did not exist. It was Monday. It ended.

Rudra had asked at the enquiry counter about the special entrance for employees. On Tuesday he entered the bank early by that entrance. But it was of no use, because, the deputy manager was in a hurry, and when Rudra asked him about how he should go about his duty, simply replied in anger that he had already told him, and walked away telling Rudra not to pester him anymore. Till Saturday which was a half working day, Rudra did nothing but stroll around aimlessly in the bank.

That Saturday, the deputy manager called Rudra into his cabin just before the bank was about to close and told him that, every Saturday those who worked directly under him stayed back after the bank closed and held a progress review meeting which he chaired.

Mr. Khanna told his employee to be present without fail at his meeting, and also asked him to bring his achievement sheet. Rudra simply nodded and left. He had no clue as to what an achievement sheet was. And there was no one he could ask as he had not struck up an acquaintance with any other employee of the bank dreading another meeting like the one with the computer operator. But he had to be present at the meeting, and he was. The meeting soon began in a small conference room after the employees who did not work directly under the deputy manager left the bank.

Rudra, who had hoped that he would not be asked for his achievement sheet, was not only disappointed but also traumatized when the deputy manager began the meeting by announcing that the new member of their team, who was his assistant, would be the first one to read from his achievement sheet.

As Rudra stood up, the floor seemed to give way beneath his feet, and he timidly said: "Sir, I am terribly sorry. I don't know what an achievement sheet is."

The deputy manager thundered:

"You don't know what an achievement sheet is! Then what work have you been doing here this entire week?"

Rudra wished that the ground would open up and swallow him as he shivered and replied:

"Nobody told me what to do, sir."

Mr. Khanna calmed down as he took pity on the miserable Rudra and said:

"First let me tell you what an achievement sheet is. It is a sheet where you enter what you have achieved that day at the end of every working day for one complete week and which you assess at the end of the week to review your progress. This is meant solely for the purpose of improving your performance and making sure that you are not slacking off in your job or taking one step behind. Understood Rudra?"

Rudra stuttered:

"Yes, sir."

Mr. Khanna continued:

"Now Rudra, I come to the most important part. There is plenty of work to be done under me. You shouldn't wait for work to come searching for you. You should go in search of work.

If you are smart, you will find that there is plenty that needs to be done. It is up to you to take the initiative. Am I clear?"

Rudra humbly replied:

"Yes, sir."

Rudra, in spite of all his conditionings, was no fool. He had common sense and guts.

Otherwise, he would not have survived for so long. He had absorbed and understood all that the deputy manager had said. During the rest of the meeting, he concentrated on understanding how the other employees under the deputy manager had gone about their duties during the week. Soon the meeting came to an end, and everybody dispersed.

Rudra spent a fruitful Sunday. His parents had called him on Monday after his first day at work. He had then told them that there was nothing much to say and that he would call them on Sunday. He did so and his voice held enthusiasm which was evident to his parents. Everybody was happy.

From the next day onwards, Rudra, after collecting the printouts the computer operator printed out, analyzed and then distributed them among the various employees who worked directly under the deputy manager and to whom they were concerned, and even sometimes suggested or made corrections himself to the contents of the printouts as far as his knowledge permitted him to do so.

The computer operator was glad that she was now free of the responsibility of calling the peon and having him deliver the printouts to whom they were concerned. To be quite frank, she was greatly relieved, because the peon's cerebral abilities were of a lower grade, and most of the times he used to come back to her with the printouts asking for instructions again. But she did not show even a little bit of appreciation to Rudra and remained aloof. However, this relief of hers was not even slightly evident to him.

For Rudra, the week flashed by, and before he knew it, it was time for the Saturday meeting. This time, he had his achievement sheet ready. But, to him, something didn't feel right even before the meeting began.

For, Nalini Iyer, the personal secretary of the manager of the bank, who didn't work directly under the deputy manager, also came to attend the meeting. But it didn't feel right only for Rudra. Only he thought Mr. Khanna alone knew the purpose of her presence at the meeting. But nobody else raised their eyebrows. There was something afoot which he didn't know about. The meeting began and everybody read out their achievement sheets. Rudra did not receive any special attention. But he was very happy that he had not been singled out and had merged with the crowd.

In the end, Mr. Khanna got up from his seat, adjusted his tie, straightened his suit, and began a speech:

"Ladies and gentlemen, please pay full and undivided attention to what I am about to say. It is an open secret that our manager is to retire on Saturday next week. Every employee will receive a circular from the manager about his impending retirement on Monday. As most of you have worked under me for several years, you very well know my mission and vision. And for those who don't know or have forgotten, I will state it once more. My mission is to become the manager of this branch before the age of fifty so that I can realize my vision in life of becoming the manager of the bank's main office in this metropolis before the age of fifty-five. I have forged all of you into a team, made you stronger, and as a result helped you to deal easily with the hardships which you face at work. And not only at work, but I have also helped you to deal with your personal traumas as well when you approached me for help. Now I ask for yours. The time has come when it will be revealed whether I get what I deserve or not. If the post of manager is filled in-house, I am sure it will be me. But if the powers that be decide to bring in a manager from outside, I will need your help. I will need every senior member of this team to write scorching emails to the powers that be opposing their action of bringing in an outsider as manager and voicing their support for me as the new manager. The junior members of this team can also write emails extolling the excellent spirited teamwork and work ethics that are present under my administration. I hope I have your support."

There was a huge cry of, "Yes sir," from the team members, and Mr. Khanna giving a thumbs-up sign said, "Thank you all very much," and left the conference room with Nalini Iyer.

Mr. Khanna's mission failed.

The emails of appreciation that the junior members of his team sent were replied to with emails cautioning them not to interfere in the administrative affairs of the bank. The scorching emails of the senior members of his team were replied to with emails asking them to resign if they had a problem with the administration, and if they wished to remain as employees of the bank, to refrain from groupism.

Mr. Khanna, who held a Master of Business Administration degree, and whose business school training had made him itch for success at every step, was left floundering. The day the new manager from outside took charge, an incident which seemed strange only to Rudra, was witnessed by him. During the lunch break, he saw Nalini Iyer crying, and Mrs. Raveena Nayak trying to console her. It was none of his business, so he did not try to pry into it. But something that had been imprinted at the back of his mind, and to which he had given no special attention before, now came to the fore.

Nalini Iyer's cubicle was just beside Mr. Khanna's cabin. It suddenly flashed before Rudra's eyes that a man used to come and sit in the bank for hours at least three to four days in a week staring at Nalini Iyer's cubicle and Mr. Khanna's cabin. Sometimes, the man used to abruptly enter Nalini Iyer's cubicle, take a pen, and come back and sit down at his seat, or leave the bank.

Rudra, who had been too busy trying to be busy, had not attached any importance to this and had simply ignored it. Therefore, it had not seemed strange to him. But now, after he had also seen Nalini Iyer attending Mr. Khanna's meeting where the deputy manager had outlined his mission and vision and asked his team for their help, something seemed fishy.

Sometimes, when strong men don't get what they have desperately longed for since long, and have put in every effort possible to achieve their dream, and their dream shatters, they go berserk. They become like bull elephants in musth. They become petty. They become vengeful. And if they cannot wreak vengeance on the person or people or system that has denied them what they had considered to be their birthright, they take out their anger on soft targets who cannot protest.

Rudra had been coming out of the black since he had been inspired by Mr. Khanna to search for work and work. He had and had made himself useful around the bank. He had merged with the crowd and was no longer the focus of attention. He had gone about his job silently.

Rudra was gaining a sense of self-worth. His addiction to darkness because of his conditionings was lessening. But the good times were about to end as quickly as they had begun. Two days after the new manager had taken charge, Mr. Khanna called Rudra to his cabin and began by saying, "Rudra, we have to meet a very important client who lives three hundred kilometers from this metropolis in a small city."

Rudra was totally in the dark as to why Mr. Khanna was telling him this and simply stood speechless. Mr. Khanna continued:

"By we, I mean Nalini, Raveena, and you along with me. Of course, only Nalini and I have to be present at the meeting, but I am taking Raveena along as well to keep Nalini company. As for you, we are going in your car. You are going to drive."

Rudra was overwhelmed by this and in a soft voice said:

"Ok, sir."

Suddenly Mr. Khanna became angry and said in a rough voice:

"Who does this manager think he is? It is his job to meet the high profile client.

Besides, the bank has given him a car like yours with a driver. He didn't even offer to let me use it to go and meet the client when I am doing his job. He needs the car simply to travel from home to the bank and back home. And he expects me to use a cheap taxi to travel to cut costs. Anyway, we leave tomorrow, stay overnight, and come back the day after. I will message you my home address. Pick me up at sharp seven A.M. and we will pick up the others on the way. You can leave now."

Rudra was still confused. It was because he had a very small ego and did not understand others with egos which were so inflated that they could burst anytime. The deputy manager had a car, but it was not as big, powerful, luxurious, or expensive as Rudra's and the one the bank had given along with a driver to the new manager. But the first thing that Rudra did after work hours was to get his car washed thoroughly.

The drive began the next morning. Rudra first picked up Mr. Khanna and then both picked up Mrs. Raveena Nayak. When all of them picked up the last member of their group, Nalini Iyer, at her house, Rudra saw the same man who spent hours at the bank many days in a week standing at the open doors of the house. He did not bother to think.

After Rudra's car had managed to escape the maddening mess of the traffic of the metropolis, and the group was cruising quite comfortably on the highway, Mr. Khanna, who was sitting in the backseat, patted Rudra's shoulder and said:

"Rudra, I believe you have not yet been introduced formally to Mrs. Nalini Iyer.

Say hello. This is Rudra, Nalini."

Rudra said hello. Mrs. Nalini Iyer also said hello.

Then, for the rest of the journey, the deputy manager, the personal secretary to the manager, and the deputy manager's computer operator, all spent the time spewing venom against the new manager and the authorities who had chosen him for the post. Thankfully for Rudra, who had not uttered a single word during the journey, it came to an end, eventually.

Rudra parked his car, and all of them, taking their light luggage, entered a hotel where they would be spending the night. Mr. Khanna approached the reception desk and asked the receptionist for one double room and two single rooms. Rudra, who heard this, was somehow not surprised. Rudra and Mrs. Raveena Nayak went to their single rooms while Mr. Khanna and Mrs. Nalini Iyer went to their double room and freshened up.

Later, they all had lunch in the restaurant of the hotel, after which Rudra drove the deputy manager and the personal secretary of the manager of the bank to the bank's high profile client's home, while Mrs. Raveena Nayak stayed behind in the hotel. Rudra waited in the car until Mr. Khanna and Mrs. Nalini Iyer came out of the house. It had been quite a long meeting which had lasted till eight P.M. When the three came back to the hotel, Mr. Khanna and Mrs. Nalini Iyer decided they would head straight for dinner. Rudra had no choice in anything, and Mrs. Raveena Nayak quickly joined them.

While they were having appetizers, Mr. Khanna, who was sitting beside Rudra, gave him a slap on the back, and laughingly said:

"I can guess what you must be thinking. I and Nalini in the same room even though I am married to someone else and so is Nalini! Listen carefully. I will tell you what others already know but don't talk about. I and Nalini are so professional that, even though we sleep in the same room on the same bed, we don't sleep with each other. Understood?"

Rudra forced a smile on his face and replied:

"Yes, sir."

Mrs. Raveena Nayak gave a laugh and said:

"I bet he hasn't."

Rudra quickly replied:

"Oh no, I have, Mrs. Nayak."

Mrs. Raveena Nayak gave a smile and said:

"You can call me Raveena, Rudra.

After all, you are now part of our private inner circle."

She then turned to Mr. Khanna and Mrs. Nalini Iyer and asked:

"Isn't he?"

Both replied at once:

"Yes, he is."

But Rudra felt he was trapped. And he was soon proved right.

The next day, they left the hotel after breakfast and reached the metropolis by lunchtime.

The two ladies were dropped off at their respective homes first, and as Rudra drove Mr. Khanna to his home, the deputy manager told him in a matter-of-fact tone of voice:

"Rudra, from tomorrow onwards you will drive me to the bank in your car in the morning and back home from the bank after working hours."

Rudra simply said:

"Yes, sir."

Rudra had no other option. From the next day onwards, he became the chauffeur of the deputy manager of the bank. A chauffeur who not only owned the car albeit one paid for with his folk's money in which he drove his master to his destinations but also was the one who paid for the fuel filled into the car to keep it running, again with his folk's money for he earned a meager salary.

Rudra was also on duty after half-day Saturdays and Sunday holidays driving Mrs. Khanna to markets and shopping malls and carrying the loads of merchandise she used to buy. The deputy manager was trying to live the life of a manager. He was a second-hand fellow.

News of Rudra's servitude spread like wildfire throughout the bank. Raveena was the first one to take advantage of it. Whenever she wanted coffee from the coffee machine, she asked Rudra to get it. He did.

Other employees of the bank were not far behind. Whenever they wanted something to eat or drink from the cafeteria, all they did was ask Rudra to fetch it for them. He did. Without complaint. But most of the time, they deliberately forgot to pay him the money he had spent in buying the food and beverages for them. But he still did not complain. As this went on, the employees went further and began asking Rudra to run sundry errands for them after working hours as well. He submitted to all these blows to his dignity without complaint, because he had been conditioned to lose his self-esteem easily without asking why, and had a morbid fear of making even the smallest of mistakes which would invoke the wrath of authority. This was not the nadir of his self-esteem. There was more to come.

Whenever the deputy manager took interviews of candidates applying for a job in the bank, he used to call Rudra into his cabin, and in front of all the aspiring candidates, give a small talk:

"Look at this fellow, Rudra. What do you think his position in the bank is?

Just a mere assistant. And he only got the job through influence. How much do you think his salary is? Just a pittance. But do you know that he lives in a posh neighborhood in this metropolis and roams around in an expensive car? However, I have made him my personal assistant in everyday affairs in addition to him working in the bank as my assistant to make him realize the value of money. He is not practical in life. I am teaching it to him the hard way. I have brought him before you all to warn you not to be like him in life. A low achiever and a person who does not respect money."

After this, Mr. Khanna used to give a pause and say:

"You can go, Rudra. You are no longer needed. I need to interview the candidates."

Rudra used to leave the cabin a broken man.

There was one more disaster. One night at two-thirty A.M. Rudra received a call from Mr. Khanna. His heart was beating wildly as he picked up the phone. Mr. Khanna came straight to the point:

"Rudra, Raveena is not performing well at the bank. I am very certain about the reason. And I also know the solution. Rudra, Raveena gave birth to a child exactly nine months after she got married. And after that, her husband lost interest in her as a sexual partner. She doesn't have a healthy sex life. Now, you are a handsome young man of her age. I think you two should get together. After all, we are a team, aren't we? Be good. Follow my advice. Good night."

Dim

Rudra barely slept that night and the nights that followed. Even in his beloved darkness. For Raveena had started acting coyly with him. And Rudra had been conditioned against becoming close to females who could be sexual partners.

Rudra's addiction to darkness for at least a quantum of solace had been lessening since he had been inspired by the deputy manager Mr. Khanna to find work and work. But, the old manager of the bank had retired and his post had been filled by an outsider. Not only the deputy manager Mr. Khanna's mission of becoming the manager of the bank had been shattered, but also the ambitious man's vision for his life had been annihilated. These circumstances had lead to unsettling disclosures and uncanny behavior by Khanna, Nalini, and Raveena which had targeted Rudra. This, in turn, had spawned abuse of Rudra's innocence, money, and time by the other employees. Khanna's phone call to Rudra in the middle of the night followed by Raveena's overtures was the last straw on Rudra's back.

Thirst for blackness had come back with a vengeance baying for Rudra's dark red blood. However, no more did Rudra find solace in the silent darkness of his home at night. He did not have his parents, the only people he was close to in his life, at his home in the metropolis. Even though he literally worshipped darkness, loneliness cast its own shadow upon his solitude, making him more miserable than he had ever been in his life.

Things came to a head one night, and Rudra after a lot of tossing and turning in his bed finally came to the conclusion that the only way out of his turmoil was to explore the metro for a place which struck a balance between his need for darkness and his new found longing to escape from its loneliness.

Therefore, once he had dropped off Mr. Khanna at his home after working hours the following day, Rudra quickly grabbed a bite to eat and began searching for a place which would have dim lighting with people around him to give him company. However, it would also have to be a place where he would be able to maintain a distance from others in it, and where nobody at any time would come over to engage him in any sort of conversation with them or ask him any questions.

Rudra made a survey of his neighborhood, and the surrounding neighborhoods for such a place, but came up empty-handed. He then began his hunt in the dingy areas far from his and other respectable neighborhoods. Rudra did not succeed that day, but his misery made him persist, and finally one night, in one of the dingy areas, he found what he was looking for.

A dingy bar almost hidden from plain sight by darkness, as there were no streetlights near it and also because the bar itself had only a single light bulb hanging in front of its entrance, shyly presented itself to the weary explorer searching for solace. One could not even read the name of the bar painted on the wall over its entrance at night. It was dimly lit inside.

Rudra began haunting that bar. There was always a crowd there. And a lot of loud babble too. Rudra could make out some conversations. Some were like where one person after getting inebriated told how he had met the country's cricket team captain in the team dressing room after a match had been won and congratulated him, following which the other members of his circle sitting at the same table, swallowing his story whole like they had swallowed the contents of many bottles of beer which lay empty before them, congratulated the drunk storyteller raucously. Rudra was not entertained by such talk. Some others drank alone. Rudra couldn't care less. However, other customers talked about the frustrations they faced at their jobs. Rudra mainly tuned into such talk. For misery loves company.

Women came to the bar with men making Rudra wonder what kind of women they must be to come to a place such as this and that too at such late hours. Rudra didn't drink alcohol. Every night he simply sat at a table, enjoyed the dim lighting, and also the conversations he tuned into. And as it happened every time, when the waiter began coming around more often to ask him for his order, he simply ordered a soft drink and sat nursing it until the bar closed. This continued for sometime after which the manager, finally losing patience with his new customer, came to Rudra's table himself and told him to order alcohol or get the hell out of the bar.

Rudra responded to this threat in his own way. He began ordering a bottle of beer along with his customary soft drink, and leaving when the bar closed with the beer bottle left unopened. The unopened beer bottle was a gift for the waiter who had served him. As a result, waiters began to compete with one another to serve him to bag the prize of a bottle of beer. This was not good for business. The manager once more came to Rudra's table and told him to drink alcohol or stay out of the bar. Rudra had no answer to this second threat. It was paradise lost for him.

The very next night, Rudra, unable to stay away from his cherished haunt, came to the dingy area and parked his car beside the bar. He got out of his vehicle and looked longingly at the dingy tavern. But it was now beyond the reach of a teetotaler like him. Rudra then looked around at the surroundings with a gnawing feeling. As usual, it was dark. There was almost a complete shroud of black over his immediate vicinity because of the paucity of sources of light nearby. But, precisely because of this, a faint glow was visible at a distance. This dim beacon enticed Rudra, and he started to move in its direction in the hope of finding another place like the one he had been rudely ejected from.

Rudra, when he finally arrived at the lighthouse which had lured him from afar, found himself on one end of a long straight street with yellow sodium lampposts lining up at equal intervals at one side of it. But the light was dim as not all the streetlights were functioning properly. On both sides of this street were derelict houses with a few floors and balconies facing it where light bulbs of various colors dimly glowed.

Rudra had seen something like this in magazines and movies. He suddenly realized he was in a red light area. The street was wide enough for some light traffic. As Rudra stood for quite some time trying to compose himself, he understood that this traffic mostly comprised of private cars and taxis in which the commercial sex workers of this street were picked up and dropped off. These vehicles were those of the moneyed who could afford hotel rooms or had their own places where they could take the women they picked up. The not so fortunate used the rooms in the dilapidated buildings on either side of the street.

The nubile females of the world's oldest profession stood leaning against the lampposts soliciting customers. Rudra started walking on the street. He was nervous because of his conditioning which warned him against having anything to do with desirable women, but he managed to overcome his nerves because of his love for dim lighting and the company of people like him who went about their own business in it. Rudra reasoned that, since these women were commercial sex workers, they were simply doing their job, and the professionals posed no threat to him. He also assumed that, since he did not expect anything from these women, they would leave him alone, as he had been left to himself in the dingy bar by the drunks. But Rudra was wrong.

No sooner had he crossed a streetlight that was working properly than a woman who was dressed seductively, and was leaning against the lamppost, called out to him:

"C'mon handsome, don't act like you haven't seen me. I can show you a very nice time."

Rudra, without stopping, hastily said, "No, thanks," and quickened his pace. Another, who was wearing skimpy clothing, and waiting at another good lamppost, whistled at him as he drew near, and said:

"Only two thousand rupees for a glimpse of heaven my man. And if you want to stay in heaven for the entire night, only three thousand more."

Rudra hurried further. The next one was like a marketing professional who said:

"Satisfaction guaranteed or your money back."

Rudra literally ran.

He stopped, beside a lamppost whose light had died, for respite. The only glow was from the bulbs in the balconies of the houses beside the street. Then he saw her. A pretty young woman dressed in a sari. Something indescribable happened to Rudra. He began staring at her open-mouthed. Rudra lost sense of time.

Rudra was roused from his reverie only when the woman said:

"Mister, take me or vacate this place.

Don't ruin my business."

Rudra stuttered a hasty sorry and unwillingly left her and the street. Something had changed in his life. He slowly walked back to his car beside the bar, and then quietly drove home, all in a daze. But Rudra was back at the street the next night. He hurriedly walked past the other commercial sex workers in his search for the particular one. Each one of the neglected ones had something to say to him.

One asked:

"Are you man enough for me?"

Another shouted:

"You must be mad to come here without money. Otherwise, why don't you pick one from so many of us?"

Yet another, laughed and said:

"You impotent drunk."

Rudra paid no heed to these insults and reached the burnt-out streetlight where he had met the one he was looking for. She was there. Rudra had gathered enough courage. In the dim light, he asked her her name. She matter-of-factly told him to do business or go away, as names were not necessary to have sex with a commercial sex worker. Rudra did not take up her offer. He quietly stood by her side until she angrily asked him to leave her alone to do her business. Rudra left.

Rudra visited the street for the third night in a row. By then, the news of his mild infatuation, with the "Lady at the Broken Streetlight," had spread among all the commercial sex workers of that street. And this time, as he walked towards the spot where she usually stood to solicit customers, he wasn't insulted by the others, instead was told by one of them that it was his unlucky day as a customer had already picked her up, and his girl would be told that he had come to meet her when she returned from her work.

She was present at her post when Rudra came to meet her on the fourth night. He silently stood beside her for more than a couple of hours. This time, she didn't chase him off.

At the end of that long wait, she said in a weak voice:

"Mister, business is down today. At least buy me a bottle of beer."

Rudra was jerked into action and happily said:

"It will be my pleasure. Let's go."

She perked up and said:

"I know a place nearby. We will go there."

Rudra agreed.

She led him to the dingy bar from which he had been expelled. When they went in through its open doors, the waiters of the tavern immediately ambushed them from all sides, each waiter asking them to come and sit at the table he was serving. The manager hurried over to the duo and welcomed Rudra, all the while apologizing that he had not known that the customer he had thrown out had what it took to be a real man. Both Rudra and the girl looked into each other's eyes with a glimmer of laughter.

Rudra said to the girl who wanted a drink:

"You must be one of their most prized customers. They never liked me before.

Now that I am with you, they are suffocating me with their respect."

She coyly replied:

"Yes, sometimes I bring my clients here before we get down to the real business.

During the times when I feel I can't be thoroughly professional, that is. But judging by what the manager said, you too are quite famous here. Have I seen you here before? I don't think so. But then, I haven't come here for a long time. Terribly busy, you know."

Rudra laughed and replied:

"Infamous, not famous. And I too have not seen you here during the time that I was tolerated in this place. I would have remembered."

She raised her eyebrows:

"Infamous?"

He said:

"Come, let us sit. You will understand."

Two bottles of beer and a soft drink were brought to their table. One bottle of beer and the soft drink bottle were opened and their contents poured into two glasses. Another bottle of beer was left unopened.

Rudra raised his glass containing the soft drink and said:

"Cheers."

The pretty young thing also raised her glass, filled with beer, in a toast.

She giggled:

"So you do not drink. That is more than sufficient to make you infamous in a bar."

Rudra smiled and answered:

"Yep. That is why I was expelled from this bar until today. After my expulsion from this institution, I started haunting your street. Lucky for me. I met you. But isn't it high time for introductions? I am Rudra, and your name is..."

The lady gave a shy smile and replied:

"Krupa."

Both then fell silent as they pondered over which subject to bring up and talk about.

It was difficult and would need one of them to relax and take the initiative. There was beer. Krupa quickly polished off her bottle of beer and was halfway through Rudra's, which had finally been opened, when she said to him:

"Let us talk about our jobs. That fancy car outside, you own it right?"

Rudra replied in the affirmative.

Krupa continued:

"You are lucky to have a job that makes it possible."

Rudra said with downcast eyes:

"My parents bought that car for me. In fact, I have a very low salaried, low-status job.

And that too acquired through my parents' influence."

His train of woe ran on:

"I was happy with my job as I do it sincerely. But lately, the boss directly above me has made my life miserable. He treats me as his chauffeur, using my car, and also as his household servant to take his wife shopping and to carry the heavy burden of all that she purchases while on her shopping spree. The other employees in the office also treat me like a peon, imitating my boss. All make me waste my parents' money. To make matters worse, my boss humiliates me whenever he gets the chance. But the most horrible thing that has taken place lately is that he wants me to sleep with his computer operator to improve her working performance, and she too has started acting coyly with me. I love my job, but this is hell."

Krupa softly exclaimed:

"Oh, my poor dear! I am so sorry to hear all this. But listen to me. Even though one can neither walk in somebody else's shoes nor put somebody else in theirs, I would like to give you some advice. You have to stand up for yourself. If I can do it, you certainly can. I got into this business at the age of sixteen. I did not know what was good for me then. My heartless pimp used to send me with all kinds of men. Many would beat me up and abuse me in myriad ways. But, by the age of nineteen, I had had enough and confronted my manager. I made it completely clear to him that whatever may be the outcome of my confrontation with him, from then on, only I would choose the customers I did business with. The cruel man threatened to disfigure my face with acid so that I would no longer be beautiful to look at. I didn't buckle under his threat and simply told him to go ahead as it would be his loss, for he would be losing one of his most beautiful employees and the high revenue she brought him. He quietly accepted my decision, as he had no guts, and was full of false bravado. I can guess with just a single look whether my prospective customer is a gentleman or a hooligan. In my line of business, very few who want my services are gentlemen. That is why my business is slow. But I only go out with gentlemen and hence am respected in my profession. Whatever that respect may mean to you."

By this time, the second bottle of beer too had become empty.

Rudra ordered a third bottle. Krupa slowly enjoyed it in silence. Once she was done with it, both left the bar together. He then dropped her back at her street in his car. Rudra didn't ask Krupa whether she would meet him the next night. She also didn't say anything except thanks and soon disappeared from sight.

Even though nothing had been promised by the girl, the boy came to meet her much before twenty-four hours had elapsed. She wasn't present. It was the same the second night in a row; the sixth night since he had first met her. But she was there again on the seventh.

However, Krupa said that she had to work as her finances were not in good shape, and asked him to go away, as she had done during their initial encounters. Rudra reacted by immediately asking her how much she charged for one night.

She replied:

"Sir, you are entering into dangerous waters. Don't do it."

Rudra quietly asked again:

"How much for one night?"

Krupa, avoiding Rudra's eyes and looking at the ground, replied:

"Five thousand rupees."

Rudra simply took out his wallet, counted out five thousand rupees, and handed it to her.

He then said:

"Let's go."

Both of them then headed to the bar with an unspoken mutual consent. Krupa gulped down an entire bottle of beer in a matter of few minutes. She then, for the first time that night, gave a smile, and said apologetically:

"I am sorry. It has been hard the two previous nights."

Rudra smiled back and said:

"It is ok."

He then ordered another bottle of beer.

This time, Krupa began to drink it slowly.

Suddenly, out of the blue, she began:

"Rudra, during the last two days and this day, during bright sunlight, when I pondered over our conversation on the night when you for the first time bought me a few beers here, I simply could not connect the dots in your story about yourself which you told me in the darkness of that night. I cannot for the life of me understand your actions.

You frequent a bar, but do not drink alcohol. Many would, if they were frustrated in their working environment, and even though you fall into that category, you don't. You come to a red light area, but don't pick up a woman for sex. Is there a girlfriend? Do you have a fiancée? Are you married? What is the matter with you? Why do you do, what you do? Why do you frequent these places? You have money. You can go to fancy clubs or star hotels instead of coming to these dingy places. Why do you not do so?"

Krupa ran out of breath.

Rudra laughed and answered:

"Alcohol does not solve problems but accentuates them. And neither am I married nor spoken for. I am still a virgin."

Rudra became serious as he continued:

"Let me tell you something. Listen to me carefully. My self-esteem is so low that I lose it easily, and also I am terribly scared of being the focus of attention, especially in a crowd. But here in this dingy bar and your red light area, the question of me becoming a pitiful victim and losing my self-esteem does not arise, as most of the people here and there are themselves pitiable and have already lost their self-esteem long ago. I feel that here I am among equals. And as to being the focus of attention in a crowd, nobody notices me in the bar here as long as alcohol is consumed at my table, by me or someone else, and in the red light area, after one or two days of soliciting and pestering, the commercial sex workers leave one alone to oneself. I am also petrified of making even a single tiny mistake that will bring down the wrath of authority upon me. But here, in these places, everything is a mistake, and neither am I the culprit nor there is any authority. Only total freedom exists. I am afraid of interacting with sexually mature females as it will lead to trouble for me, but amidst commercial sex workers where sex is just like any other business, a business which I am not looking to conduct, I do not expect to find any trouble. In these places, there is nothing for me to feel ashamed about or be afraid of. Understood Krupa?"

Krupa was into her third bottle of beer.

She raised her glass and said:

"Cheers. You are quite an item, sir. There definitely cannot be another piece like you in this world. God doesn't make the same mistake twice."

She then gave a hearty laugh and continued:

"Please don't mind, sir. I was just joking. But I still feel that the most significant piece of the puzzle is missing."

Rudra gave a sigh:

"Yes. I come to these places for the company which does not bother me."

Krupa didn't swallow it:

"No. That is not it. There is something else that you are not telling me."

Rudra ordered a fourth bottle of beer for Krupa and succumbed:

"Alright. You are right. I love the darkness. I come to these places for the dim light in which everything is set. I do it so that I can lose myself in the darkness. I love it because in this dim light one appears beautiful to oneself when one looks into a mirror. In this dim light, all your flaws are obscured. You reign supreme."

Krupa, taking a sip from the fresh bottle of beer, accepted:

"Now, that makes sense."

After this closure, Rudra talked about his family, and Krupa told him how lucky he was to have such parents while she had been forced into prostitution by hers to make ends meet. When Rudra said that he was sorry to hear about her parents being so inhuman, Krupa simply replied:

"They are what they are. They are the ones who deserve pity. Not me. Anyway, let's stop talking about my parents. I want to enjoy my beer."

Both sat in silent satisfaction and Krupa finished her last beer.

Then Rudra dropped her off with the words:

"Goodnight. Have a good rest."

Krupa was happy:

"Thanks to you I will. Goodnight."

Both then went their separate ways.

Unshackled

Something magical had happened to Rudra. The troubled human had owned up to his weaknesses in front of someone. That someone, was Krupa, a human opposite to him in every respect, and the power which had made that magic happen to him was the love which had blossomed in his heart for her. An unconditional love which not only went against all of society's norms but which had also set out to conquer society's conditionings. Once one owns up to and faces one's weaknesses, they cease to be one's weaknesses.

It was a different Rudra who came to the bank the next day. Rudra had not picked up the deputy manager from his home or his phone calls on the way to the bank. And when a fuming Mr. Khanna arrived late at the bank and demanded to know the reason for his assistant's indiscipline, Rudra simply replied that he and his car would not be at his boss's disposal anymore.

Mr. Khanna's bloated and fragile ego burst, but he could not ask why. However, beginning from that day, a raging anger against Rudra started building up deep inside of him. From that day onwards, Rudra also began turning a deaf ear to the absurd requests by the other employees of the bank asking him to perform actions which were not part of his job description. This first made them feel helpless, then humiliated, and finally insanely angry at Rudra. But they could not do anything about it.

But Mr. Khanna could, and he did. One day, when he could not bear what he considered to be blatant insubordination by Rudra anymore, he hired a private detective to watch his activities. During the weekends, Rudra had begun to take Krupa out for lunches, movies, theme parks, and other fun-filled bright places.

When Krupa had initially asked why he was crawling out of his comfort zone of dim lighting, Rudra had replied that her happiness during daytime when she did not have to work overshadowed his conditioning seeking comfort in the late evening. Then, when Krupa had probed further and asked him whether he was trying to impress her, he had replied in the affirmative. The commercial sex worker had been scared to ask why, fearing that she would lose the company offered to her by a good human being, with no strings attached, and simply began to enjoy the pleasant moments with him.

Meanwhile, Rudra, who had fallen in love with her, was scared to express his love for her as he did not know whether the commercial sex worker was capable of accepting it or not, even though his love was unconditional and it would not matter to him if she did not reciprocate the feeling. So, both went ahead with their indescribable relationship.

The private detective clandestinely watched Rudra's activities day and night. When the dirty sleuth had gathered enough dirt against Rudra, he presented his findings to the deputy manager. They were innocent if seen in the proper light. But, Mr. Khanna's eyes and mind were clouded by an anger which had reached saturation level because of what he considered to be betrayal by someone to whom he had done a great favor.

Even the anger of the other employees of the bank at Rudra, because of what they considered to be his audacity, had exceeded the boiling point. The findings of the detective, which Mr. Khanna distributed among others who shared his rage against Rudra, were sufficient to spur them into action. Everybody combined in a conspiracy to get Rudra fired from his job at the bank.

The plot was hatched, and then the deputy manager, with the other employees backing him up in the conspiracy against Rudra, told the new manager of the bank that the old manager had employed Rudra without advertising the vacancy of the post now held by him in any newspaper, and also without conducting any sort of interview. And, that Rudra had only got the job through influence. Rudra was immediately fired from his post as assistant to the deputy manager of the bank. Rudra was relieved. Justice had prevailed.

But the vengeance of the wounded did not end. Mr. Khanna called up Rudra's parents and told them that the bank had to fire Rudra on moral grounds as their son consorted regularly with a commercial sex worker, and that all the other employees had signed a petition seeking his dismissal.

Rudra's parents were shocked beyond words. However, they immediately called up their son, and somehow managed to ask him whether Mr. Khanna had spoken the truth. The pained husband and wife were somewhat soothed when their only offspring told them that what Mr. Khanna had said about him was true, but that they had heard only one side of the story and not the whole truth.

The confused couple, gathering courage, told their

progeny that they would immediately come to the metropolis and settle his problems. When Rudra's parents reached his home in the metropolis, they expected to see a dejected young man; someone with a dejection that had been an integral part of their son when he had been growing up. But to their great and pleasant surprise, their son was literally glowing when he welcomed them into his home. It was evening.

Rudra ordered dinner from outside and told his parents to have patience and eat well before he began his story. His parents found the roles reversed and were patient. Dinner arrived quickly, and it was consumed even more quickly, for anticipation, a powerful master, was in the air.

Once everybody made themselves comfortable in the living room, Rudra began his story in the metropolis from scratch and ended on a high note. His parents listened carefully with mixed feelings. But in the end, all they could feel was only love for their son.

Rudra's father, softly placing a hand on his son's shoulder, gently said:

"Don't worry son, whatever decision you take, we will support you."

Rudra was calm as he spoke:

"I have a few requests, father. Take away this car. I want my old moped back. I don't want to live in this house. I want to stay as just a paying guest in some decent area. I want to find a job on my own merit. Also, I would like to do a postgraduate course through distance education."

His father, without any questions, said:

"Ok son. You are now ready to face the world. I respect

all your decisions."

The young man's father and mother had tears of joy in their eyes when they hugged their son before going to sleep. They left the metropolis the next afternoon after arranging for a driver to drive them in their son's car, back to their home in the city.

Rudra, whose love bound him to the metropolis, searched the newspapers for a decent place to stay as a paying guest, and also job interviews for which he was qualified. He soon found a good place to stay, and his moped arrived by train to the metropolis. But, the graduate didn't get any good job interviews, for his experience as assistant to the deputy manager of a bank didn't count simply because his previous employers had given him no certificate of experience.

Finally, Rudra had to settle with being a clerk in the finance section of a newspaper office. However, he had wasted no time and had started studying very hard for a Post-Graduate Diploma in Business Administration through distance education choosing Human Resource (HR) as his specialization. He had chosen HR because he had empathy.

Rudra's target was to get his postgraduate diploma in the shortest time possible and get a good job. Rudra's conditionings and obsessive-compulsive disorder were a thing of the past now. An unconditional love for someone who had made him see how fortunate he was, had completely erased without a trace all that which would have otherwise shackled him to a life of abject misery. Rudra began to meet Krupa only on Sunday mornings. He had decided that he would let her know of his love for her only when he got a good job after finishing his postgraduate course.

Rudra felt that, even if she did not love him, or she did but was unable to express it openly, he would be happy if she simply and patiently participated in their present relationship until he told her of his unconditional love for her. However, whatever Rudra might have decided or felt, in harsh reality, Krupa, whether she loved him or not, had no choice or say in the whole matter.

Rudra's father had accepted the fact that Krupa, the commercial sex worker, was now a permanent part of his son's life. And his son's life was their family's life. So he coaxed his son's mother, who had not yet fully digested the idea of her son's life having a commercial sex worker in it, to accept their son's decision. Soon, she too, along with her husband, began asking about Krupa whenever the couple talked with their son on the phone.

Love

Rudra took three years, to get his postgraduate diploma, three months, to land a decent job in a multinational company, and a day, an anxious first at his new job, to tell Krupa that he loved her when he came that night to meet her. She had waited for him for she had known he would come that night.

Rudra was not worried that his love would be rejected by the commercial sex worker. He only wanted to give and did not expect anything in return. However, the time they had spent together on Sunday mornings for three years and three months had provided adequate testimony of her commitment towards their indescribable relationship. Rudra felt that even if Krupa's love for him at present was absent, it would bloom soon, thereby making her happier in life and their relationship. He was already the happiest man in the world.

Krupa had been severely abused by life. It had been a harsh three years and three months for her. She had had to ply her trade every night in order to keep poverty at bay while Rudra had been slogging away at his small-time job and studies. The only pleasure that Krupa had got from life during those three years and three months had been in the form of Rudra, and that too, a Rudra who had stopped splurging his parents' money and had entertained her in the only way he could; by taking her for walks in gardens on beautiful Sunday mornings and treating her to snacks in restaurants on those pleasant Sunday afternoons

All the nights, she had had to suffer in her trade. She had felt Rudra was suffering too. Hence, Krupa had been left wondering why Rudra didn't live the life his parents had once gifted him with and which he had forsaken, and whether he really cared about her or not, as he had left her to ply her business at night, when he could easily have rescued her from it.   She had saved enough, by working horrifying extra hours and limiting everything else to a bare minimum, to secure her freedom from her pimp, but could not afford to start a fresh life without somebody there to support her as she knew no other way to pay her bills.

Krupa knew that Rudra knew it. But he had never told her that he loved her, and she herself couldn't quite grasp that precious feeling of what it was to be in love. Therefore, that night when Rudra told her he loved her, Krupa trembled as she posed a question:

"Why now after knowing each other for so many years during which nothing has happened?"

Rudra was silent for a moment before he grimly answered:

"It takes time for one to become a man. To express his love for a woman.

A woman if she accepts his love becomes a mother to their children. For a woman is meant to be a mother. And the man, the family's provider. I have taken the decision that I want to spend my life with you. For now, I can provide for our present and future with my own effort. During our suffering, such a decision was impossible to take. But it had to be taken in due time, and I have now. That's why."

Rudra, with clear eyes, added:

"Now that I have presented my case, the ball is in your court."

Krupa, without meeting Rudra's eyes, cautiously asked him:

"What do you see in me?"

Rudra carefully replied:

"It doesn't matter. Not that you are not pretty, but love is blind. Don't ask me to explain why. I can't. Furthermore, there are two reasons why I am expressing my love for you only now. The primary reason is that I am no longer scared of you rejecting my love as our companionship has lasted for a harsh three years and three months without either one of us voicing any kind of expectation from the other. The secondary reason lies in the self-confidence that I have finally gained after this hiatus of three years and three months during which I slogged and became a man from a youngster.

Now I have the confidence of a man who can support a family on his own. I don't expect you to have the same feelings for me immediately. But I will be incredibly happy if you just agree to spend the rest of your life with me. The house of love is just. It opens its doors to all those who knock on them. I have knocked and found love. I am waiting for you to knock. I am sure you will and that you too will find love. I have found it in you and I am more than certain you will find it in me someday. Of course, we will both have to change some of our habits and attitudes if we are to stay happily together, forever. But it will be a small price to pay for love which is priceless. Now, will you marry me?"

Krupa, meeting Rudra's twinkling eyes, with tears in hers, happily said:

"Yes."

Krupa was as self-reliant, if not more, than Rudra, and therefore without asking for help from him, immediately got rid of the manager of her old business with the money she had saved for a life of freedom. When Rudra informed his parents about the latest developments, they said:

"Bring her home son."

He did. Rudra and Krupa had the blessings of his parents.

Real Education for Life began.

www.ingramcontent.com/pod-product-compliance
Lightning Source LLC
LaVergne TN
LVHW091614170726
843492LV00007B/2399